Night Walk

Story by Jill Newsome
Illustrations by Claudio Muñoz

MYRIAD BOOKS LIMITED

To Liliana –
and to all dog and cat lovers

MYRIAD BOOKS LIMITED
35 Bishopsthorpe Road, London SE26 4PA

First published in 2002 by
ANDERSEN PRESS LTD
20 Vauxhall Bridge Road,
London SW1V 2SA

Published in Australia by Random House Australia Pty.,
20 Alfred Street, Milsons Point, Sydney, NSW 2061

ISBN 1 905606 15 X

Printed in China

Outside in the garden,
the blackbird sings
her morning song.
Flute the cat and
Daisy the dog
wake up.

Daisy rushes wildly upstairs,
    while Flute, stretching and yawning,
        just ignores her.

Breakfast is ready . . .

. . . then out for a walk.

But Flute just wanders
and waits for the quiet
while Daisy is out.

Now she is ready for breakfast . . .

. . . and her stroll in the garden.

She loves sniffing around and
having the house all to herself.

"You smell different," she says to Daisy.
"I've been to the park with the rabbits and the squirrels,"
answers Daisy.
"What are rabbits and squirrels?" asks Flute.
"Well . . ." thinks Daisy aloud, "a rabbit is like a giant mouse
with very long ears, and a squirrel is . . . a sort of rat
with a fluffy tail who lives up in a tree."

"Hmm . . ." wonders Flute,
"they don't sound very nice to me.
Do you like them?"
"In a way," replies Daisy, ". . . I do."

This evening the moon is shining and Daisy is going for a night walk.
"A night walk?" thinks Flute. "That sounds interesting."

She loves the night
but has rarely been beyond
the garden gate.

Bravely stepping out,
she follows them up the road.

"Oh, good!" says Daisy.
"Let's go to the park together!"
"The park? Oh, dear!"
says Flute.

The night is full of
too many strange smells
and noises, but worst of all . . .

But Daisy is there in an instant to frighten them all away.

Staying close together,
they reach the gates of the park.
"Oh, dear!" says Flute.
"What an enormous place!"

Daisy dashes off, chasing
a shadow into the night.
Flute rushes up
the nearest tree.

Two large eyes
peer out of the dark.
"Good evening!
And what can I do for you?"
"Oh, dear!" says Flute.

She dives into the bushes below.
"Hello," says a voice.
"Are you a friend of Daisy?"
"Oh, dear!" says Flute.

Two strange animals appear in the moonlight.
But before she has time to answer,
Owl screeches above them.
"Help! There's trouble ahead. Follow me!"
As they run, a distant dreadful din gets louder and louder,
and what they see stops them in their tracks.

"Oh, dear!" say Badger and Fox. "It's Wildcat!"
"Oh, no!" shouts Flute. "It's Daisy!"

Hissing and spitting, she charges forward.
"Hey, you big brute! Leave my friend alone!"

"Flute!" gasps Daisy.

The little band of new-found
friends closes in.
"Yes, Wildcat," they demand.
"Why are you being so beastly?"

"Your friend came too close," Wildcat growls,
"and I'm only defending my babies."
Four little faces peep through the brambles.
"I'm so sorry, Wildcat," says Daisy. "I didn't see
them there and I only wanted to play."

So one by one the kittens come out to play.

Then the time comes to go back home.

"You were so brave!" says Daisy. "What would I have done without you?"

Flute just smiles.

Good night, Daisy!
Good night, Flute!